D1394799

*Bangers and Mash are two naughty chimps
who live with Mum, Dad and Gran at
number 3 Tree Street, Chimpton. You can read
about their amazing adventures in the books in
this series.*

British Library Cataloguing in Publication Data

Groves, Paul
  Ghost boast.
  I. Title   II. McLachlan, Edward, *1940–*   III. Series
823′.914 [J]
  ISBN 0-7214-1222-X

First edition

Published by Ladybird Books Ltd Loughborough Leicestershire UK
Ladybird Books Inc Auburn Maine 04210 USA

© LADYBIRD BOOKS LTD MCMLXXXIX
© LONGMAN GROUP UK LTD/FILMFAIR LTD MCMLXXXIX

*All rights reserved. No part of this publication may be reproduced, stored in a retrieval
system, or transmitted in any form or by any means, electronic, mechanical, photo-copying,
recording or otherwise, without the prior consent of the copyright owners.*

Printed in England

Bangers & Mash
Ghost boast

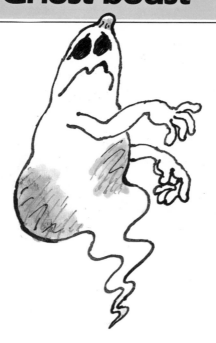

by Paul Groves
illustrations by Edward McLachlan

Ladybird Books

All was quiet in the tree house at number 3 Tree Street, Chimpton, where Bangers and Mash live with Mum, Dad and Gran.

The cheeky chimpanzees were out. They'd gone to play in the squelchy mud down by the pond.

"Lovely mud!" said Bangers.

"Lovely mess!" said Mash.

They were soon covered in mud, but when it was time to go home they decided to take some back with them. They sloshed it into their buckets and set off.

It was a good job that Mum couldn't see them. She wouldn't have been very pleased.

As Bangers and Mash were
carrying the mud home, along
came their friend, Petal.

Bangers says she is
called 'Petal'
because she is like
a flower –
a cauliflower.

Mash says she is like
a flower too –
a bag of plain flour.

When they got to number 3 Tree Street, they all settled down on the step to make mud pies.

Unfortunately they dropped one, just as Gran was walking along the path. It hit her on the head and slopped down her face.

"Never mind, Gran," said Bangers. "Ladies put mud on their faces to make them beautiful."

Mum didn't want Gran to have beauty treatment.

"Go and tell her you're sorry!" she shouted. "Clean the mud off the step. Have a wash. Then go and play somewhere else. And make sure it's a nice clean game!"

So Bangers and Mash and Petal said "sorry" to Gran. They washed the mud off their hands and faces and rode their bikes down to the pond.

But they completely forgot to clean the step. There were mud pies all over it.

The chimps reached the muddy pond. There was a little house on the other side of the reeds, made from a bit of old drainpipe. It was the home of Mrs Snitchnose.

Mrs Snitchnose was a witch and she didn't like the cheeky chimps.

But that didn't bother Bangers and Mash. "Let's pay her a visit," said Bangers. So Bangers, Mash and Petal rode round and round the witch's house calling her names.

Mrs Snitchnose soon lost her temper. "I'll teach them!" she said, and reached for her broomstick.

The chimps pedalled off as fast as they could. Mrs Snitchnose taxied down her runway. She gained speed, lifted up her underskirt – she was off!

First Petal was in the lead,
then Bangers, then Mash. Then
Mrs Snitchnose nearly caught them
but the road forked suddenly
and Bangers and Mash turned left
and Petal turned right.

That confused Mrs Snitchnose. She
went straight on and got lost in the
trees.

In the end, she went into reverse
and flew back to her house.

Bangers and Mash were in for a spell of trouble, now!

That night, when they were safely tucked up in bed, Mrs Snitchnose flew off to the gloomy old house that only witches know about.

There, she made a spell. A wobbly white ghost came out of the floorboards.

The ghost rode behind
Mrs Snitchnose all the way to
number 3 Tree Street.

She put it down on the doorstep
and told it what to do. "Get in
through the letterbox," she said.
"Go upstairs and frighten those
two naughty chimps."

"O-Oh," sniggered the ghost, "I'll
frighten them out of their skins."

So the wobbly white ghost got
ready to slither through the
letterbox. *Crash!* It slipped on the
mud pies that Bangers and Mash
had forgotten to clean up. It
banged its head on the front door.

"Oh! Oh! Oh!" it moaned. But
the chimps stayed fast asleep.

The ghost flew up to the roof. It squeezed down the chimney and slid down into the kitchen.

There, on the table, was a pile of banana sandwiches. Bangers had made them in case they needed a midnight snack.

The greedy ghost couldn't resist banana sandwiches.

But Bangers hadn't bothered to peel the bananas. The skins gave the ghost a very bad tummy ache.

"Oh! Oh! Oh!" it moaned.

"What's that?" said Bangers, waking up.

"Nothing," said Mash. "Go back to sleep."

When it felt a bit better, the ghost crept upstairs – there were Bangers and Mash lying fast asleep.

The ghost stuck its chest out and cleared its throat.

At last it was ready to do some haunting.

The ghost decided to give Mash
the first fright.

It slid into his bed and settled
down. But there was a hot water
bottle in the bed.

"Oh! Oh! Oh!" it moaned,
leaping up. But Bangers and Mash
stayed fast asleep.

Now ghosts do not like hot things.
It leaped out of the bed and
hovered in the air.

It turned round to
look over its
shoulder. And it
could just see a
big burn on its
bottom.

The ghost was now in a very
bad temper. It went to
Mrs Snitchnose's house and said,
"Just look at me!"

So Mrs Snitchnose looked. The
ghost seemed very colourful.

On its head was a
big purple bump.
That came from
falling on the
step.

There was a green
patch on its
tummy. That came
from eating the
banana skins.

Its bottom
glowed red. That
came from sitting
on the hot water
bottle.

"I give in!" said the ghost.
"I want my beauty sleep."
And it climbed straight into
Mrs Snitchnose's bed.

"That's my bed!"
said Mrs Snitchnose.

"Not tonight
it isn't!"
answered the
ghost.

"But where am
I to sleep?"
cried the witch.

"On the floor!"

The ghost rubbed its purple bruise, stroked its green tummy, and patted its red bottom. Then it stretched out in bed, gave a snore and fell fast asleep.

Mrs Snitchnose was furious!

Back at number 3 Tree Street, Bangers and Mash were *still* fast asleep. They didn't even wake up for their midnight snack.

Later that night, a strange noise *did* wake Bangers – but only for a moment.

"What was that?" he squeaked.

"Only the duck on the pond!" muttered Mash. "Go to sleep!"

Later on, another eerie noise woke Mash – but only for a second.

"What's that?" he whispered.

"Only an owl hooting!" murmured Bangers. "Go to sleep!" And he did.

But Mrs Snitchnose didn't get a wink of sleep all night. Well, it's not very nice, is it, having to sleep on the floor?